Dear Parent:

Congratulations! Your child is taking the first steps on an exciting journey. The destination? Independent reading!

STEP INTO READING® will help your child get there. The program offers five steps to reading success. Each step includes fun stories and colorful art. There are also Step into Reading Sticker Books, Step into Reading Math Readers, Step into Reading Write-In Readers, Step into Reading Phonics Readers, and Step into Reading Phonics First Steps! Boxed Sets—a complete literacy program with something for every child.

Learning to Read, Step by Step!

Ready to Read Preschool–Kindergarten
• **big type and easy words** • **rhyme and rhythm** • **picture clues**
For children who know the alphabet and are eager to begin reading.

Reading with Help Preschool–Grade 1
• **basic vocabulary** • **short sentences** • **simple stories**
For children who recognize familiar words and sound out new words with help.

Reading on Your Own Grades 1–3
• **engaging characters** • **easy-to-follow plots** • **popular topics**
For children who are ready to read on their own.

Reading Paragraphs Grades 2–3
• **challenging vocabulary** • **short paragraphs** • **exciting stories**
For newly independent readers who read simple sentences with confidence.

Ready for Chapters Grades 2–4
• **chapters** • **longer paragraphs** • **full-color art**
For children who want to take the plunge into chapter books but still like colorful pictures.

STEP INTO READING® is designed to give every child a successful reading experience. The grade levels are only guides. Children can progress through the steps at their own speed, developing confidence in their reading, no matter what their grade.

Remember, a lifetime love of reading starts with a single step!

For Annie, Margaret, and Po—M.M.-K.

Special thanks to Vicki Jaeger, Monica Okazaki, Tanya Mann, Christine Chang, Rob Hudnut, Shelley Dvi-Vardhana, Jennifer Twiner McCarron, Pat Link, Shawn McCorkindale, Walter P. Martishius, Tulin Ulkutay, and Ayse Ulkutay

Published in the United States by Random House Children's Books, a division of Random House, Inc., 1745 Broadway, New York, NY 10019, and in Canada by Random House of Canada Limited, Toronto.

Visit us on the Web!
www.stepintoreading.com
www.barbie.com

Educators and librarians, for a variety of teaching tools, visit us at
www.randomhouse.com/teachers

Library of Congress Cataloging-in-Publication Data
Man-Kong, Mary.
Barbie and the three musketeers / adapted by Mary Man-Kong ; based on the original screenplay by Amy Wolfram.
    p. cm. — (Step into reading. Step 2)
ISBN 978-0-375-86007-2 (trade) — ISBN 978-0-375-96007-9 (lib. bdg.)
I. Dumas, Alexandre, 1802–1870. Trois mousquetaires. II. Title.
PZ7.M31215Bar 2009 [E]—dc22 200855167

Printed in the United States of America
20 19 18 17 16 15 14 13 12

STEP INTO READING®

STEP 2

Barbie™ and The Three Musketeers

WITHDRAWN

Adapted by Mary Man-Kong

Based on the original screenplay by Amy Wolfram

Illustrated by Ulkutay Design Group and Allan Choi

Random House 🏠 New York

Corinne loves to fence.
She wants to be
a Musketeer.
She wants to protect
the royal family.

Corinne goes to Paris.
She learns that she
cannot be a Musketeer.

A dog chases
Corinne's kitten.
Corinne runs after them.
They splash past Viveca.

Corinne bumps
into Aramina.

Renée falls

into the water.

Corinne finds her kitten near the castle.

Corinne meets the girls she splashed, bumped, and knocked over! They forgive her.

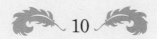

Corinne gets a job
at the castle.

She is a maid.

She meets Prince Louis.

He is going to be king.

Philippe is Louis's cousin.

Philippe is angry.

He wants to be king.

Prince Louis is
in danger.

<u>Crash!</u>

The roof caves in!

Corinne smashes rocks.

Viveca cracks bricks.

Aramina kicks stones.
Renée breaks blocks.
Everyone is saved!

The girls want
to protect the prince.

They want to be
Musketeers!
They use a secret room
to practice.

Prince Louis takes
his hot-air balloon
for a ride.
But someone cut the rope!
Corinne saves Louis.

Corinne and the prince
float over Paris.
They have fun together.

Philippe plans
to attack Louis.

The girls have a plan, too.
They will protect the
prince.

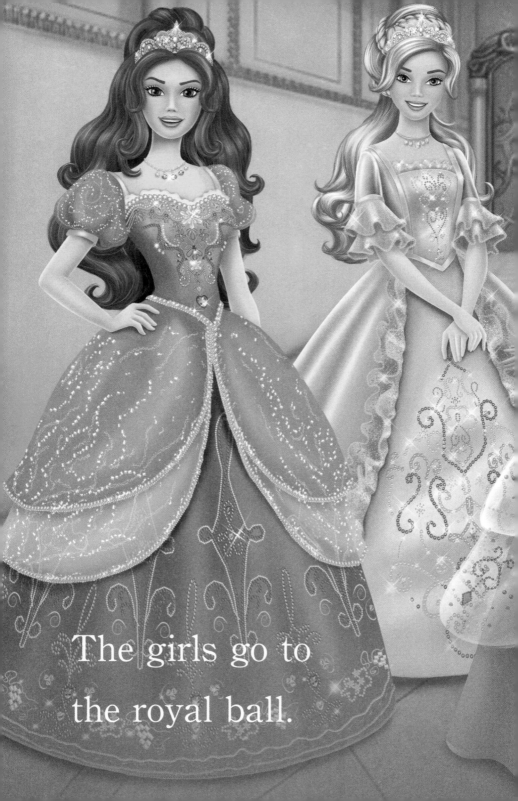

The girls go to
the royal ball.

Their gowns sparkle.
Their crowns shine.

Corinne dances
with the prince.

Philippe is going
to attack the prince!

The girls are ready!

Corinne uses her sword.
Viveca uses her ribbons.
Aramina uses her fans.

Renée uses her bow.

They stop the attack!

Corinne stops Philippe
with her sword.
The prince is safe!

Louis makes all
the girls royal
Musketeers.

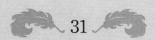

All for one
and one for all!